Little, Brown and Company

Hachette Book Group
237 Park Avenue, New York, NY 10017
Visit our website at lb-kids.com

LB kids is an imprint of Little, Brown and Company.
The LB kids name and logo are trademarks of Hachette Book Group, Inc.

The publisher is not responsible for websites (or their content) that are not owned by the publisher.

First Edition: March 2014

Library of Congress Cataloging-in-Publication Data

Sisler, Celeste.
Pixie Hollow bake off / adapted by Celeste Sisler. — First edition.
pages cm. — (Disney fairies)
Summary: Tink challenges Pixie Hollow's best bakers to a bake off, with the winning cake to be featured at Queen Clarion's Arrival Day party.
ISBN 978-0-316-28332-8
[1. Fairies—Fiction. 2. Bakers and bakeries—Fiction. 3. Contests—Fiction.] I. Title.
PZ7.S621952Pix 2014
[E]—dc23

2013041752

10 9 8 7 6 5 4 3 2 1

CW

Printed in the United States of America

Disney FAIRIES

PIXIE HOLLOW BAKE OFF

Adapted by Celeste Sisler

LITTLE, BROWN & COMPANY
LB kids

Fairies from all over Pixie Hollow have come to see Tinker Bell and her friends take on the baking fairies in a contest to bake a cake for Queen Clarion's Arrival Day celebration.

"Welcome to the first-ever Pixie Hollow Bake Off," Bobble shouts as Clank enters Pixie Hollow Stadium in a balloon.

"Let's meet the competitors, shall we, Clankie?" Bobble asks.

"Presenting...the baking fairies," shouts Bobble. "Led by Gelata!"

"Baking is my life," Gelata says, smiling. "For the last three hundred ninety-nine years, we, the baking fairies, have made the same perfect mouthwatering cake. Do you think we will get to four hundred? Piece of cake."

She looks over at her competition and winks. "A little baking humor," she whispers. Gelata knows she will win.

"Versus..." yells Bobble, "the non-baking fairies! Led by Tinker Bell."

Tinker Bell had suggested shaking things up in the kitchen this year: perhaps a pink cake instead of a white one. Somehow that resulted in Tink leading a team in her first-ever bake off.

"I'm not too worried," says Tink with a shrug. "I mean, isn't baking just tinkering with flour?"

Tinker Bell thinks this will be easy.

"Game on," Gelata says.

"You have one hour to bake, chefs," says Bobble. "And your time starts"—Clank sets the timer to sixty minutes—"NOW!"

Tink spreads out her cake design on the table. The fairies gather around.
"Okay, so it's a six-tiered cake," says Tink, "in which we will visually tell the entire history of Pixie Hollow."
The fairies nod enthusiastically.

On the other side of the kitchen, Gelata slaps down her blueprint of a perfectly mapped-out cake.

"The usual," Gelata says. The baking fairies nod. They know exactly what they need to do. They have done it 399 times before.

Gelata unrolls her chef's bag, revealing her perfectly ordered baking tools.

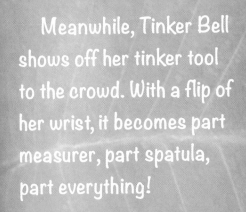

Meanwhile, Tinker Bell shows off her tinker tool to the crowd. With a flip of her wrist, it becomes part measurer, part spatula, part everything!

Step Three: The Dry Ingredients

Gelata effortlessly juggles her flour and sugar. She gives a dash here and a shake there. The baking fairies work as an organized assembly line.

On the other side of the kitchen, Tink uses a giant tinkered mixing device to sift her ingredients together. As the mixture shoots into the air, the girls catch it in thimbles.

Gelata combines the dry and liquid ingredients with ease. Tinker Bell mixes water with her dry ingredients in a nutshell. She gives Gelata a carefree expression. She is feeling a win for the non-baking fairies.

Step Five: The Transfer

Once the batter is mixed, Gelata tosses her pans in the air. Her baking fairies catch them and swiftly set them in the oven to bake.

Step Six: The Baking

Iridessa stands in front of the table with her team's cake layers. She uses her light talent to quickly bake the cake!

Gelata moves down the line of ovens as the baking fairies reveal one perfect cake layer after another. "Sensational...scrumptious...yum," Gelata says.

Step Seven: The Final Preparations

"It's down to the home stretch," Bobble announces. "It's do-or-die time."

The baking fairies frost their cake to perfection, and then Gelata checks to make sure each layer is perfect.

WHOOSH! Vidia zooms around the cake and carves it, giving it a unique shape. Tink and the girls rush to finish frosting and decorating.

"Attention, bakers," Bobble yells. "Whisks down in five, four, three..." The baking fairies are already lined up to present their finished cake. One baking fairy yawns.

Tinker Bell and the girls work up to the last second!
They are tired and covered in ingredients but happy with
their cake.

"Hands up! Utensils down!" Bobble shouts. "And now
for the judging! Remember, contestants are evaluated on
presentation and taste. Baking fairies, your cake."

Queen Clarion walks up to sample the baking fairies' cake.

"Ah, beautiful as usual," she says. Then she takes a bite. "Delicious... as usual."

Gelata is pleased with herself and her team. She gives Tinker Bell a smug look.

Bobble invites Tink and the girls to present their cake to the
queen. They carefully set it on the table.

"It's the most...unusual cake I've ever seen," says the queen.

The fairies are nervous. Does the queen like it?

She pauses for a moment and then claps her hands together.
"I love it!" she says.

The girls are so happy. They think they have already won.
"All that remains is the tasting," says Bobble.
Everyone crowds around as Clank and Bobble prepare
a slice for the queen to taste.

Queen Clarion brings the piece of cake to her mouth,
and as soon as she tastes it, her eyes pop open in shock.
Something is terribly wrong. What does it taste like?

The results are in! Gelata's cake is the winner!

Clank and Bobble take Tinker Bell and Gelata aside for a post-baking interview.

"So, we lost on taste." Tink frowns. "But at least I made a point to Gelata."

Gelata responds, "Will I shake things up? Absolutely. In fact, for cake number four hundred one, I have decided to make our frosting half a shade whiter!"

Tinker Bell laughs—at least she tried!

Host your very own bake off—just like Tinker Bell and Gelata!
Decorate six cupcakes with white or green frosting, and use these
cupcake toppers to identify Team Tink and Team Gelata.
Have a taste test to see who wins! (Or is it a tie?)

Team Gelata!

Team Gelata!

Team Gelata!

Team Tink!

Team Tink!

Team Tink!